It is early **morning**.
The sun is rising.
It's time for Zara Zebra
to wake up.

It is **late morning**.
The sun has risen.
It's time for Zara Zebra
to go shopping.

It is the **middle of the day**.
The sun is high in the sky.
It's time for Zara Zebra to eat lunch.

It is **afternoon**.
The sun is setting. The moon is rising.
There's still time for Zara Zebra to play.

It is **evening**.
The moon is high
in the sky.
It's time for Zara Zebra
to read a book.

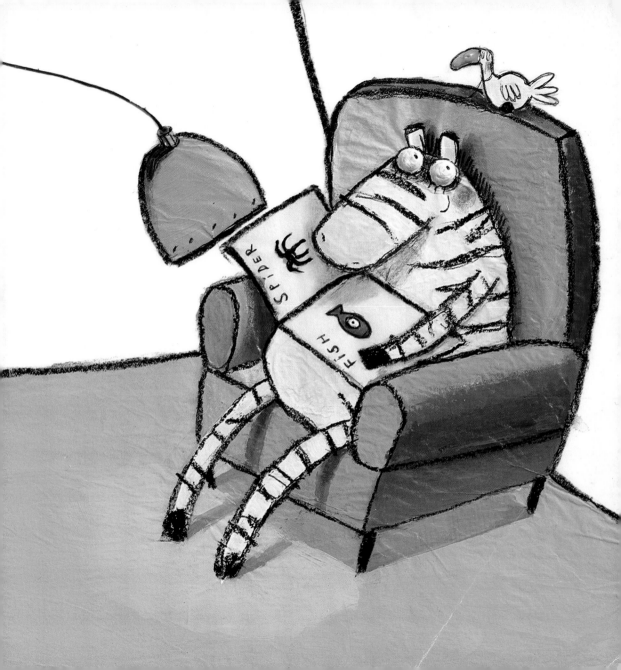